W9-DFR-057

FEB 1 5 2007

North Palm Beach Public Library

DEMCO

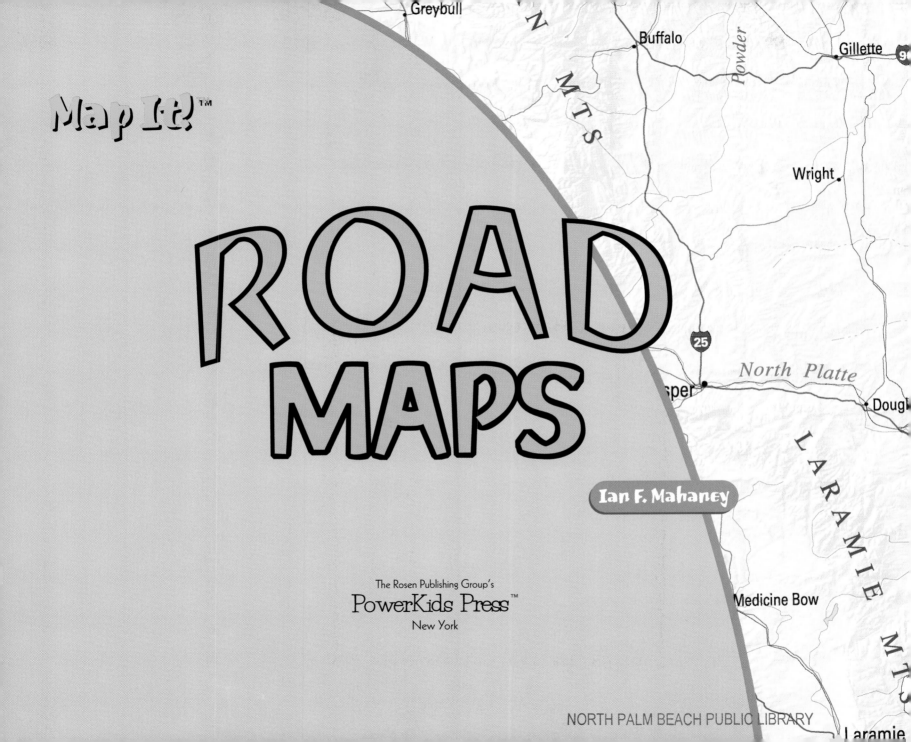

ROAD MAPS

Map It!™

Ian F. Mahaney

The Rosen Publishing Group's
PowerKids Press™
New York

NORTH PALM BEACH PUBLIC LIBRARY

To my parents, who still deal with me daily

Published in 2007 by The Rosen Publishing Group, Inc.
29 East 21st Street, New York, NY 10010

Copyright © 2007 by The Rosen Publishing Group, Inc.

All rights reserved. No part of this book may be reproduced in any form without permission
in writing from the publisher, except by a reviewer.

First Edition

Editor: Jennifer Way
Book Design: Greg Tucker
Photo Researcher: Jeffrey Wendt

Photo Credits: Cover (left), p.1 © Royalty-Free/Corbis; cover (right), pp. 1, 5, 9, 10, 13, 14, 17, 18 National Atlas of the United States,
http://nationalatlas.gov; pp. 6, 18 (inset) © 2002 GeoAtlas; p. 21 © AAA, used by permission.

Library of Congress Cataloging-in-Publication Data

Mahaney, Ian F.
  Road maps / Ian F. Mahaney.
      p. cm. — (Map it!)
  Includes index.
  ISBN 1-4042-3056-4 (lib. bdg.) — ISBN 1-4042-2212-X (pbk.)
1. Map reading—Juvenile literature. 2. Roads—Maps—Juvenile literature. I. Title. II. Series.

GA130.M363 2007
912'.014—dc22

                                            2005028986

Manufactured in the United States of America

Contents

What Is a Map?

Maps are everywhere. They help us understand the world in which we live. Do you know how to use a map? Do you know what a map is?

A map is an **illustration** of a place. A map helps us understand the world around us. Maps use **symbols**, colors, and lines to show the map's features. Maps usually have three things. First maps usually have a **legend**. This explains the symbols used on the map. Maps also usually have a **scale**. A scale tells you how distances on the map compare with distances in the real world. Finally most maps have a **compass rose**. A compass rose shows you the four main directions. They are north, south, east, and west. This book will teach you how to use a road map.

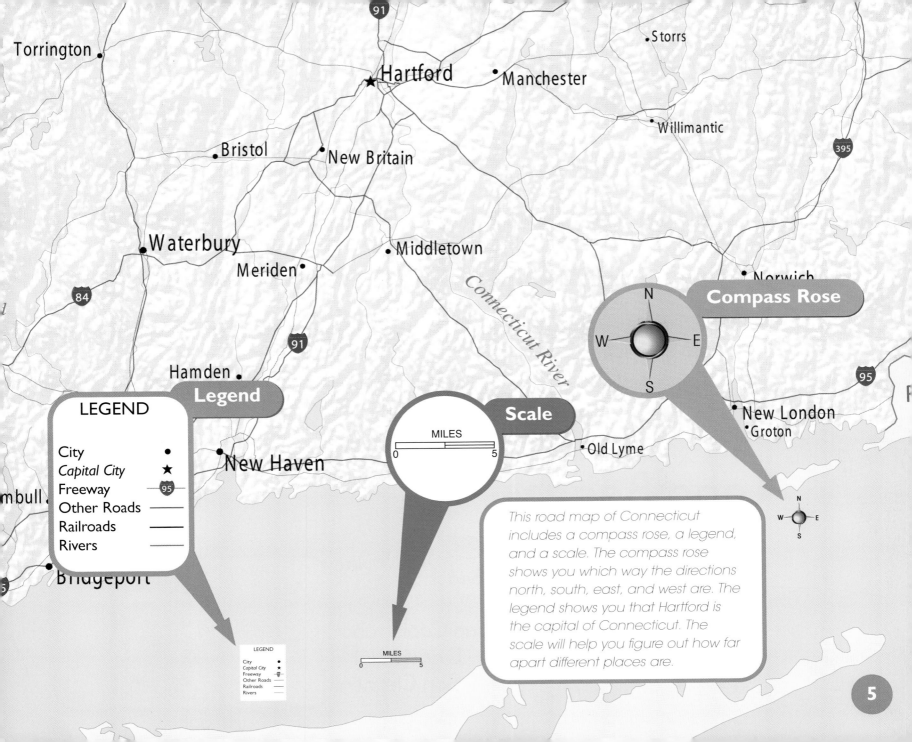

Torrington

Hartford ★
Manchester

Storrs

Willimantic

Bristol
New Britain

395

Waterbury
Middletown
Meriden

84
91

Connecticut River

Compass Rose

N
W   E
S

Norwich

Hamden
Legend

LEGEND

City   •
Capital City   ★
Freeway   95
Other Roads   —
Railroads   —
Rivers   —

New Haven

MILES

0   5

Scale

Old Lyme

95

New London
Groton

N
W   E
S

This road map of Connecticut
includes a compass rose, a legend,
and a scale. The compass rose
shows you which way the directions
north, south, east, and west are. The
legend shows you that Hartford is
the capital of Connecticut. The
scale will help you figure out how far
apart different places are.

Bridgeport

LEGEND

City   •
Capital City   ★
Freeway
Other Roads   —
Railroads   —
Rivers   —

MILES

0   5

Sespe Cr.

S

Ojai

Quartz Hill

Santa Paula   Fillmore   Santa Clarita

ra

Moorpark

Oxnard

Simi Valley

San Fernando

Thousand
Oaks

Burbank

Glendale   Pasadena

Beverly Hills

Los Angeles

Santa Monica ✈

Whittier

Inglewood ✈

Downey

Compton

Torrance ✈

Norwalk

Fullerton

Anaheim

Long Beach

Huntington Beach

✈ Irvine

Newport Beach

San Juan Capistrano
Dana Point
San Clement

Santa Catalina I.

Fallbrook

Mojave

D   e

Victorville

App

Hesperi

Crestline

Ontario

Pomona

Rialto

San Be

Mentor

Riversi

Norco
Corona

Yucaipa

10

215

▲3506

Large City   ○

Small City   ○

Urban Areas   🌫️

Interstate Highway 🛡️80

Major Highway   ———

Local Road   ———

Airport   ✈

River   〰️

On this road map of the Los
Angeles area, you can see the
different roads, such as interstate
highways, that lead to the city. The
map also shows the airports and
other cities. Road maps help you
choose routes and navigate
between places.

What Is a Road Map?

When people travel in the United States, it is usually by roads and streets. Road maps show how the system of roads is built and how to use different roads to get where you are going. Road maps help you navigate, or drive in the correct direction.

Roads maps show **physical** and natural features to help you better understand the area through which you are traveling. Oceans, rivers, lakes, and forests may be shown on road maps. Road maps also show many humanmade objects, such as **highways**, cities, or airports. Makers of road maps accomplish all this by drawing lines on the map that **represent** roads and by using symbols to **identify** the humanmade objects and natural features that appear on the map. Once you learn how to read these lines and symbols, you will be able to use a road map.

One of the most important parts of a road map is the legend. The legend will help you understand the symbols on a road map. Road maps use three types of symbols. They are point symbols, area symbols, and line symbols.

Point symbols are used to identify fixed points such as cities. Area symbols are used to identify larger things, such as lakes. For example, a lake would be colored blue. The legend also includes line symbols. Line symbols stand for features such as roads, railroads, or rivers. The thickness, the pattern, and the color of the lines are what make these symbols stand out. Learning to use the legend will help you understand road maps. Look at the legend on the right. You will find examples of point, area, and line symbols.

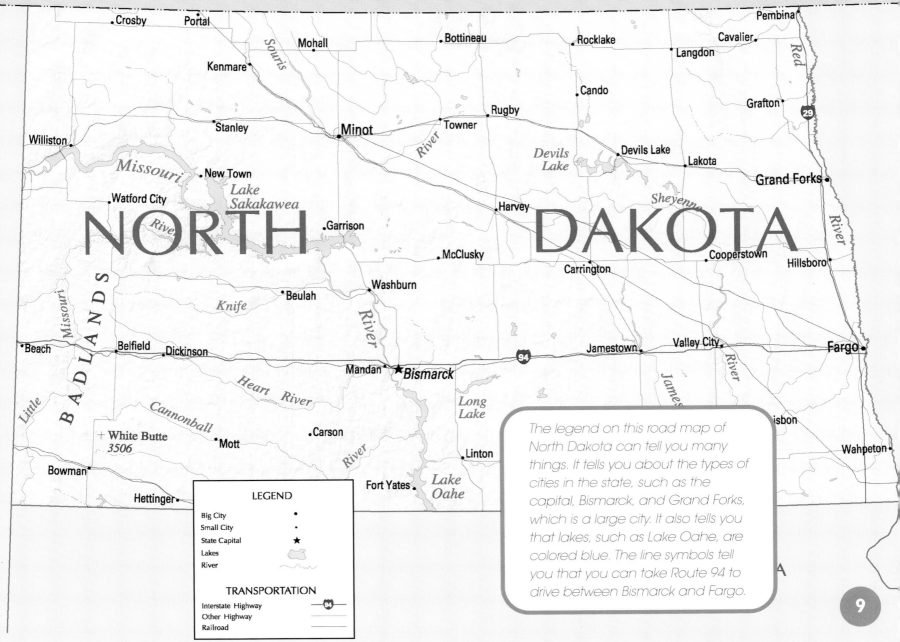

CANADA

NORTH DAKOTA

Crosby • Portal •
Mohall •
Bottineau •
Rocklake •
Pembina •
Cavalier •
Langdon •

Kenmare •
Cando •
Grafton •

Souris River

Williston •
Stanley •
Minot
Towner •
Rugby •
Devils Lake •
Lakota •
Grand Forks •

Missouri River
New Town •
Lake Sakakawea
Devils Lake

Watford City •
Garrison •
Harvey •
Sheyenne River
Cooperstown •
Hillsboro •

McClusky •
Carrington •

Knife River
Beulah •
Washburn •

BADLANDS

Missouri

Beach •
Belfield •
Dickinson •
Jamestown •
Valley City •
Fargo •

Heart River
Mandan •
★ Bismarck
94
James River
isbon •

Little Missouri

Cannonball
Carson •
Long Lake

+ White Butte 3506
Mott •
Linton •
Wahpeton •

Bowman •
Fort Yates •
Lake Oahe

Hettinger •

LEGEND

Big City •
Small City ·
State Capital ★
Lakes
River

TRANSPORTATION

Interstate Highway ─94─
Other Highway
Railroad

The legend on this road map of North Dakota can tell you many things. It tells you about the types of cities in the state, such as the capital, Bismarck, and Grand Forks, which is a large city. It also tells you that lakes, such as Lake Oahe, are colored blue. The line symbols tell you that you can take Route 94 to drive between Bismarck and Fargo.

9

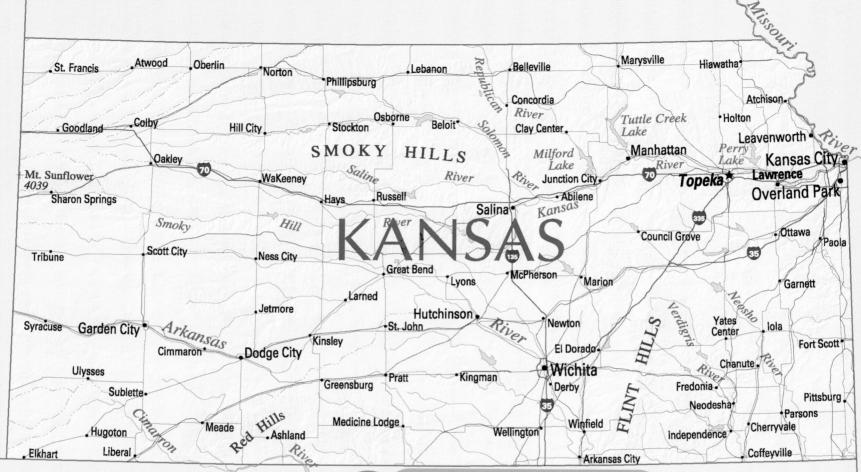

KANSAS

SMOKY HILLS

FLINT HILLS

Red Hills

Rivers: Missouri River, Republican River, Solomon River, Saline River, Smoky Hill River, Kansas River, Arkansas River, Cimarron River, Neosho River, Verdigris River, Red Hills River

Cities and places:
St. Francis, Atwood, Oberlin, Norton, Phillipsburg, Lebanon, Belleville, Marysville, Hiawatha
Goodland, Colby, Hill City, Stockton, Osborne, Beloit, Concordia, Clay Center, Atchison
Mt. Sunflower 4039, Oakley, WaKeeney, Holton, Leavenworth
Sharon Springs, Hays, Russell, Salina, Manhattan, Junction City, Abilene, Topeka, Kansas City, Lawrence, Overland Park
Tribune, Scott City, Ness City, Great Bend, McPherson, Marion, Council Grove, Ottawa, Paola
Larned, Lyons, Garnett
Jetmore, Hutchinson, Newton, Yates Center, Iola, Fort Scott
Syracuse, Garden City, Kinsley, St. John, El Dorado, Chanute
Cimarron, Dodge City, Pratt, Kingman, Wichita, Fredonia, Pittsburg
Ulysses, Greensburg, Derby, Neodesha, Parsons
Sublette, Medicine Lodge, Winfield, Independence, Cherryvale
Hugoton, Meade, Ashland, Wellington, Arkansas City, Coffeyville
Elkhart, Liberal

Tuttle Creek Lake, Milford Lake, Perry Lake

LEGEND

Big City	•
Small City	.
State Capital	★
Lakes	
River	

TRANSPORTATION

Interstate Highway	━
Other Highway	──
Railroad	──

Building Your Knowledge

Look at this road map. Imagine you want to travel from Topeka to Lawrence. Notice that there is more than one route that will take you there. One route uses a major freeway, another uses a smaller road. Using the legend, figure out which route would probably get you from Topeka to Lawrence faster. Which road would you choose?

Using the Legend

Until you are comfortable reading common symbols on a road map, the map's legend will help you understand these symbols. The map's legend is usually in a box on the side of a map.

Many symbols in the legend are the same from map to map. Major roads like interstate freeways are usually labeled with thick red lines. Other roads, like state freeways, are shown with a thinner red line. Even smaller roads may be labeled with thin black lines. Dirt roads may be shown as broken lines. It can be hard to understand all these lines crossing over each other. The basic rule is, the thicker the line, the bigger the road. Keeping this rule in mind can help you choose the best **route** to get someplace when you are using a road map.

Understanding Direction

Earlier we talked about the compass rose and how it shows the directions north, south, east, and west on the map. Look at the road map of Florida on the right. Find the compass rose. It has four arrows that are marked N, S, E, and W. The arrow that points up is labeled with an N. This shows north. The arrow pointing down points south. The arrow pointing left points west, and the arrow pointing right points east.

Using directions we can compare the positions of two cities. Can you find the cities of Jacksonville and Orlando on the map? Jacksonville is near the top of the map, and Orlando is near the middle. If you place your finger on Jacksonville and slide your finger toward Orlando, you move your finger down. Moving down on the map is south. This means that Orlando is south of Jacksonville.

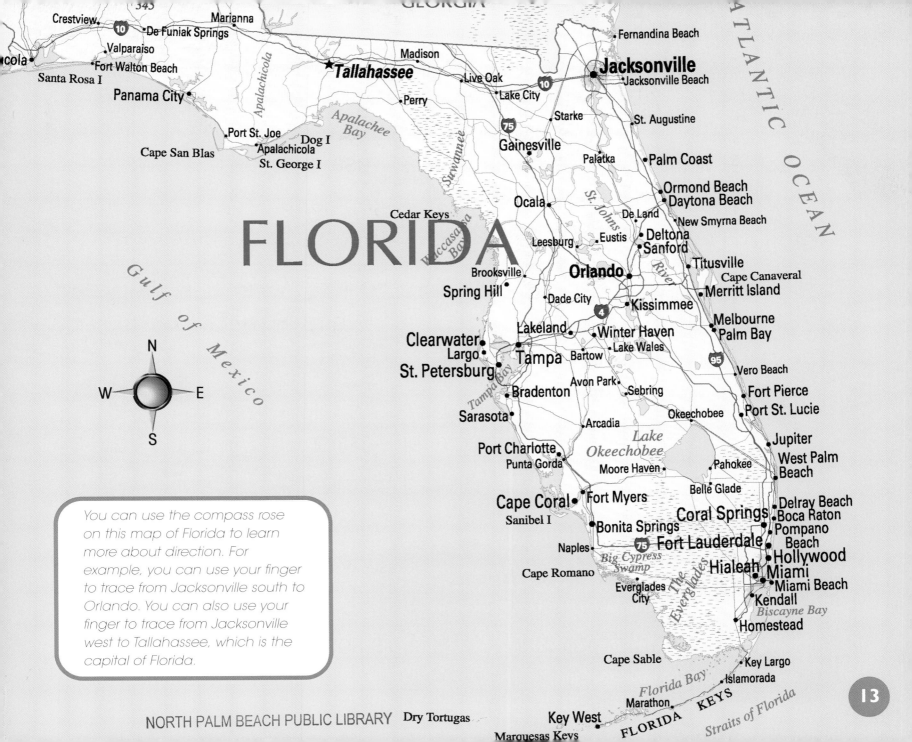

GEORGIA

343

Crestview • ⑩ • De Funiak Springs Marianna
cola Valparaiso Madison
• Fort Walton Beach ★**Tallahassee** • Live Oak • Fernandina Beach
Santa Rosa I • Lake City **Jacksonville**
Panama City • • Perry • Jacksonville Beach
⑩
Port St. Joe • *Apalachicola* ⑦⑤ • Starke • St. Augustine
Cape San Blas • Dog I *Apalachee* • Palatka
Apalachicola *Bay* **Gainesville** • • Palm Coast
St. George I

Cedar Keys **Ocala** • • Ormond Beach
  • De Land • Daytona Beach
FLORIDA • New Smyrna Beach
Leesburg • • Eustis • **Deltona**
  • Sanford
Brooksville • **Orlando** • Titusville
Spring Hill • • Dade City • Cape Canaveral
④ • Kissimmee • Merritt Island
Lakeland **Melbourne**
Clearwater • • Winter Haven • Palm Bay
Largo • • Lake Wales
Tampa Bartow • ⑨⑤
St. Petersburg • • Vero Beach
  Avon Park • • Sebring • **Fort Pierce**
Bradenton • • Port St. Lucie
Sarasota • • Arcadia Okeechobee •
  • Jupiter
Port Charlotte • *Lake* • **West Palm**
Punta Gorda • *Okeechobee* **Beach**
  Moore Haven • • Pahokee
  • Belle Glade • **Delray Beach**
Cape Coral • Fort Myers • **Boca Raton**
Sanibel I **Coral Springs** • • **Pompano**
Bonita Springs **Beach**
Naples • ⑦⑤ **Fort Lauderdale** • **Hollywood**
  Big Cypress • **Hialeah** • **Miami**
Cape Romano • *Swamp* • Miami Beach
  Everglades *The* • Kendall
  City *Everglades* *Biscayne Bay*
  • **Homestead**

Cape Sable *Florida Bay* • Key Largo
  • Islamorada
NORTH PALM BEACH PUBLIC LIBRARY Dry Tortugas Marathon **FLORIDA KEYS**
Key West *Straits of Florida*
Marquesas Keys

Suwannee River *St. Johns River* *Waccasassa Bay* *Tampa Bay*

Gulf of Mexico

ATLANTIC OCEAN

N
W   E
S

You can use the compass rose on this map of Florida to learn more about direction. For example, you can use your finger to trace from Jacksonville south to Orlando. You can also use your finger to trace from Jacksonville west to Tallahassee, which is the capital of Florida.

13

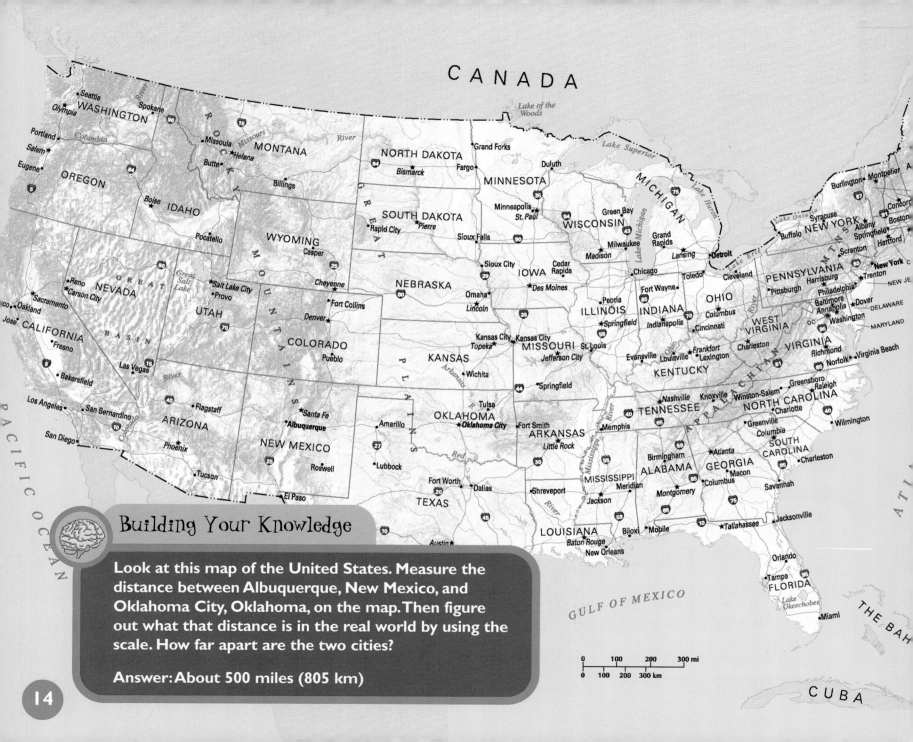

CANADA

Seattle · Spokane
Olympia ·
WASHINGTON
Portland ·
Salem ·   Columbia   River
Eugene ·
OREGON   Missoula ·   Missouri   River
                Helena ·
                Butte ·   MONTANA
Boise ·   Billings ·
IDAHO
Pocatello ·   WYOMING   Casper ·
Reno ·   Great   Salt   Lake
Carson City ·   Salt Lake City ·
NEVADA   Provo ·
Sacramento ·   UTAH
Oakland ·
co · Oakland   BASIN   Cheyenne ·
Jose ·   Fort Collins ·
CALIFORNIA   Denver ·
Fresno ·   COLORADO
                        Pueblo ·
Las Vegas ·   River
Bakersfield ·
Los Angeles ·   Flagstaff ·   Santa Fe ·
San Bernardino ·   ARIZONA   Albuquerque ·
San Diego ·   Phoenix ·   NEW MEXICO
                                Roswell ·
                Tucson ·
                        El Paso ·

NORTH DAKOTA   Grand Forks ·
Bismarck ·   Fargo ·   Duluth ·
                MINNESOTA
SOUTH DAKOTA   Minneapolis ·
Rapid City ·   St. Paul ·   WISCONSIN   Green Bay ·
Pierre ·   Milwaukee ·   Grand Rapids ·
Sioux Falls ·   Lansing ·
Sioux City ·   IOWA   Cedar Rapids · Chicago ·   Toledo ·
NEBRASKA   Des Moines ·   Fort Wayne ·   OHIO
Omaha ·   Peoria ·   INDIANA Columbus ·
Lincoln ·   Springfield ·   Indianapolis · Cincinnati ·
Kansas City · Kansas City ·   ILLINOIS
Topeka ·   MISSOURI St. Louis ·   Evansville ·   Louisville · Lexington ·
KANSAS   Jefferson City ·   Frankfort ·
                Wichita ·   KENTUCKY
                Springfield ·   Nashville · Knoxville ·
                Tulsa ·   Memphis ·   TENNESSEE
Amarillo ·   OKLAHOMA   ARKANSAS
                Oklahoma City · Fort Smith ·
                                Little Rock ·
Lubbock ·
        Red   River   Shreveport ·   MISSISSIPPI
Fort Worth ·
Dallas ·   Jackson ·   Meridian ·   ALABAMA
TEXAS   Birmingham ·
                                                Montgomery ·
Austin ·
                                                LOUISIANA   Biloxi · Mobile ·
                                                Baton Rouge ·
                                                New Orleans ·

Lake of the Woods   Lake Superior
Lake Michigan   MICHIGAN   Lake Huron
Lake Erie   Lake Ontario   Cleveland ·   PENNSYLVANIA
Detroit ·   Pittsburgh ·
                                NEW YORK   Buffalo ·   Syracuse ·   Albany ·
                                        Harrisburg ·
WEST   VIRGINIA   Philadelphia ·
VIRGINIA   Charleston ·   Richmond ·   Baltimore ·
                                Norfolk · Virginia Beach · Annapolis · Dover
                                                DELAWARE
                                                MARYLAND
Burlington · Montpelier ·
Concord ·   Boston ·
Springfield · Hartford ·
Scranton ·   New York ·
                NEW JE
DC · Washington ·
                Winston-Salem · Greensboro · Raleigh ·
                NORTH CAROLINA Charlotte ·
                Greenville ·
                Columbia ·   Wilmington ·
                SOUTH
                CAROLINA   Charleston ·
                Atlanta ·
                GEORGIA Macon ·
Columbus ·   Savannah ·
                Jacksonville ·
Tallahassee ·
                Orlando ·
                Tampa ·
                FLORIDA
GULF OF MEXICO Lake Okeechobee
                Miami ·

PACIFIC OCEAN

ATL

THE BAH

CUBA

Building Your Knowledge

Look at this map of the United States. Measure the distance between Albuquerque, New Mexico, and Oklahoma City, Oklahoma, on the map. Then figure out what that distance is in the real world by using the scale. How far apart are the two cities?

Answer: About 500 miles (805 km)

0   100   200   300 mi

0   100   200   300 km

Understanding Scale

A road map illustrates part of the world. It is printed onto a piece of paper. To be able to show a large area on a piece of paper, mapmakers use a scale. The scale is a line with bars and numbers written at either end. The scale shows that a certain distance on Earth is equal to a certain length on the map.

Look at the scale on the left. If you measure the length of the line between the bars of the scale, that space is 1 inch (2.5 cm). The bar on the left is labeled 0 miles (0 km) and the bar to the right is labeled 300 miles (483 km). That means that on this map, 1 inch (2.5 cm) is equal to a distance of 300 miles (483 km) in the real world. Use the scale to figure out the distance between Detroit and New York City. On the map they are about 1.7 inches (4.3 cm) apart. That means the two cities are about 500 miles (805 km) apart in the real world.

Sometimes you might have trouble finding a place on a road map. You can use the **index** to help you. The index lists the locations on the map. Each location is a combination of a letter and a number. These letters and numbers are arranged on the edge of the map.

Look at the road map of Ohio on the right. Imagine you want to find the route between Athens and Bellefontaine. Imagine you are having a hard time locating Bellefontaine on the map. You can use the index to look up Bellefontaine. The index says Bellefontaine is at C-3. Find the letter *C* on the top of the map. Now find the number 3 on the side of the map. Trace a finger from *C* and a finger from 3 until your fingers meet. This will show you where Bellefontaine is on the map.

Index

A
Akron F-2
Alliance F-2
Ashland E-2
Ashtabula G-1
Athens E-5

B
Barberton E-2
Beavercreek B-4
Bellefontaine C-3
Bucyrus D-2

The index is an alphabetical listing of locations that are found on a map. Look at the index on this page. It tells you that the city of Bellefontaine is located at C-3. Athens is at E-5. Using the index can help you find places more quickly on a map.

A B C D E F G

1 2 3 4 5 6

Lake Erie

Ashtabula
Toledo
Euclid
Lorain
Sandusky
Cleveland
Fremont
Elyria
Parma
Strongsville
Warren
Norwalk
Cuyahoga Falls
Kent
Youngstown
Fostoria
Akron
Findlay
Barberton
Alliance
Ashland
Canton
Bucyrus
Wooster
Massillon
Mansfield
East Liverpool
Scioto
Marion
New Philadelphia
Steubenville
Bellefontaine
OHIO
Mt. Vernon
Coshocton
Westerville
Cambridge
Upper Arlington
Gahanna
Newark
Springfield
Columbus
Zanesville
Dayton
Kettering
Beavercreek
Lancaster
Middletown
Circleville
Hamilton
Washington Court House
Athens
Fairfield
Chillicothe
Cincinnati
Hillsboro
Jackson

DIANA
PENNSYLVANIA
KENTUCKY
Muskingum River
River
Ohio River
Portsmouth
Gallipolis
Ironton

17

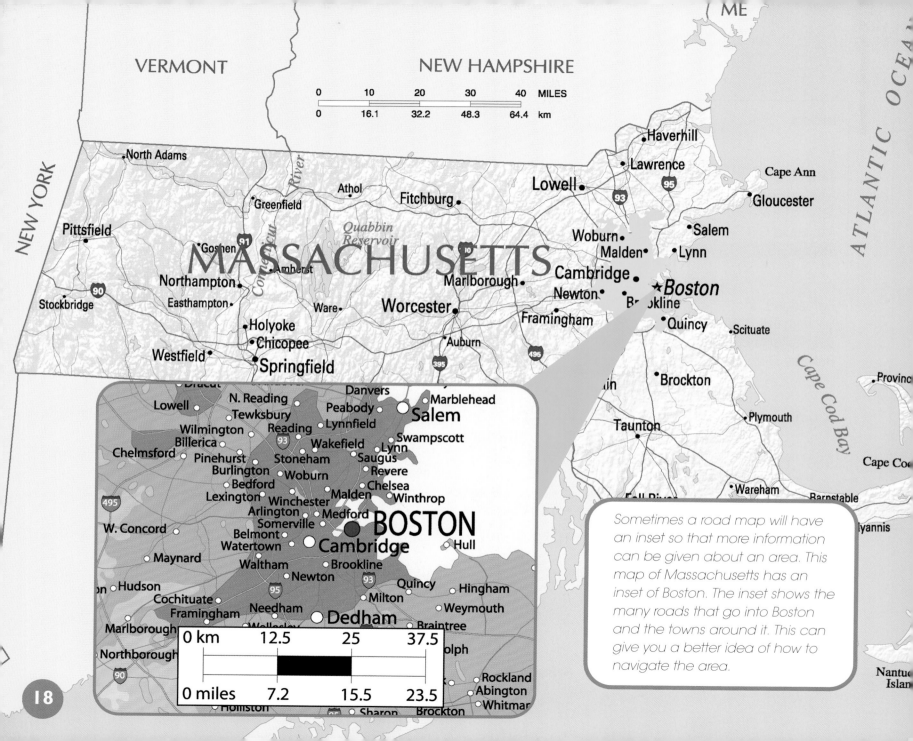

VERMONT

NEW HAMPSHIRE

ME

0   10   20   30   40   MILES
0   16.1   32.2   48.3   64.4   km

ATLANTIC OCEAN

NEW YORK

North Adams

•Haverhill

Cape Ann

•Lawrence
95

Lowell

•Gloucester

Greenfield

Athol

Fitchburg

93

Pittsfield

Woburn

•Salem

91

Goshen

90

MASSACHUSETTS

90

Malden

•Lynn

Cambridge

Northampton

Amherst

Marlborough

★Boston

Easthampton

Newton

Brookline

Stockbridge

Ware

Worcester

Framingham

•Quincy

•Scituate

Westfield

Holyoke
•Chicopee

Auburn

495

•Brockton

•Provinc

Springfield

395

Taunton

•Plymouth

Cape Cod Bay

Cape Cod

•Wareham

Barnstable

Lowell

Danvers

N. Reading

•Marblehead

Tewksbury

Peabody

Salem

Wilmington

Reading

Lynnfield

Swampscott

Billerica

Wakefield

Lynn

Chelmsford

Pinehurst

Stoneham

Saugus

Burlington

Woburn

Revere

•Bedford

Chelsea

Lexington

Winchester

Malden

Winthrop

Arlington

Medford

BOSTON

Somerville

Belmont

W. Concord

Watertown

Cambridge

•Hull

Maynard

Waltham

Brookline

Newton

93

Hudson

95

Quincy

•Hingham

Cochituate

Milton

Framingham

Needham

•Weymouth

Marlborough

Dedham

•Braintree

Northborough

90

Rockland
Abington
Whitman

Wellesley

Sharon

Brockton

Holliston

Fall River

yannis

Nantuc
Islan

0 km   12.5   25   37.5

0 miles   7.2   15.5   23.5

Sometimes a road map will have an inset so that more information can be given about an area. This map of Massachusetts has an inset of Boston. The inset shows the many roads that go into Boston and the towns around it. This can give you a better idea of how to navigate the area.

Detailed Road Maps

The main part of a road map includes most of what you need to know when you are planning a trip. Big cities, however, often have many roads going through them, and that can be hard to show if the map shows a large area. Mapmakers sometimes show these areas on separate, smaller maps within the larger map. The detailed map has its own scale and sometimes includes its own legend.

Look at the two maps to the left. The larger map is the map of Massachusetts. There is not much **information** about the roads that go through Boston in this map. The map inside the box shows the Boston area. Notice that this map has a separate scale. It shows many smaller roads into and around Boston and includes more details.

The back side of a road map also includes useful information. The back sometimes includes a detailed map like the one you learned about in the last chapter. The back side of the map can also have maps of other areas, such as state parks or national forests. The back may also include details about public **transportation**, such as buses or subways. These features are all useful to people who are traveling to the area. The back side of a map may also provide you with important information. This can include phone numbers for the fire department or the police department.

Road maps are often used to help travelers on vacation. You can use a road map to help guide you while traveling. The back of the map can give you information you can use once you arrive.

TOLL FACILITIES

Schedules and/or operation and fares of toll facilities shown on this map are subject to change or cancellation without notice. Space limitations preclude the printing of complete ferry schedules. Check with the local AAA/CAA club for complete information.

FERRIES

Inside Passage/Coastal Pacific Ocean

Juan de Fuca Strait

Port Angeles, WA-Victoria, BC: Ferry. Daily service, year round, except 2 weeks in Jan. Car and driver $30; RVs under 18 ft. $30, over 18 linear ft. $2.75 per foot. Passengers: adult $8, child (5 - 11) $4.

Port Angeles, WA-Victoria, BC: Passenger ferry. Late-May - Oct. 1. Round trip: adult $20 - $25, seniors (65+) $18 - $25, child (5 - 11) $10.

Puget Sound

Bremerton-Seattle, WA: Ferry. All-year, daily service. Car to $10; pickup-camper, trailer or RV by length; adult

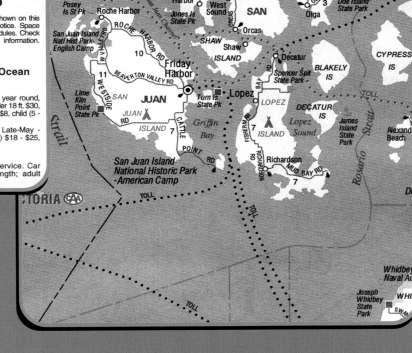

These are just a few things that are on the back of a road map of the Seattle-Tacoma area. For example, there is information about ferries, which are boats that travel between islands and the mainland (above). The back of the map also has an index (background) to help you find places such as parks, schools, and museums.

The Road Maps of Tomorrow

Road maps help you plan a trip. You can also find the locations of places to eat and gas stations along the way. By learning how to use a road map, you can figure out how long your trip will take. You can plan rest stops along the way.

There have been **innovations** in mapping. GPS is a tool that helps travelers plan their routes. GPS stands for Global Positioning System. It shows users exactly where they are located. GPS works using **satellites**. The satellites send information to the GPS tool that tells a user his or her exact location. Sometimes a GPS can even display a road map on its screen. This is a different way to use a road map. By using a GPS tool in addition to using the map-reading skills you have learned, you can plan trips faster and better than ever before.

Glossary

compass rose (KUM-pus ROHZ) A drawing on a map that shows directions.

highways (HY-wayz) Large, new roads.

identify (eye-DEN-tuh-fy) To tell what something is.

illustration (ih-lus-TRAY-shun) A picture that helps explain something.

index (IN-deks) A list, usually found at the back of a map, that states what is on the map and where a location can be found.

information (in-fer-MAY-shun) Knowledge or facts.

innovations (ih-nuh-VAY-shunz) Creations of new things.

legend (LEH-jend) A box on a map that tells what the figures on the map mean.

physical (FIH-zih-kul) Having to do with natural forces.

represent (reh-prih-ZENT) To stand for.

route (ROOT) The path a person takes to get somewhere.

satellites (SA-tih-lyts) Spacecraft that circle Earth.

scale (SKAYL) The measurements on a map compared to actual measurements on Earth.

symbols (SIM-bulz) Objects or pictures that stand for something else.

transportation (tranz-per-TAY-shun) A way of traveling from one place to another.

Index

A
airports, 7
area symbols, 8

C
cities, 7–8, 19
compass rose, 4, 12

D
detailed maps, 19–20
directions, 4, 12
dirt roads, 11

G
GPS (Global Positioning
   System), 22

I
index, 16
interstate freeways, 11

L
lakes, 7–8
legend, 4, 8, 11, 19
line(s), 7–8, 15
line symbols, 8

P
point symbols, 8

R
railroads, 7–8
rivers, 7–8
route, 11, 16

S
scale, 4, 15, 19
state freeways, 11
state parks, 20
symbols, 4, 7, 11

Web Sites

Due to the changing nature of Internet links, PowerKids Press has developed an online list of Web sites related to the subject of this book. This site is updated regularly. Please use this link to access the list:

www.powerkidslinks.com/mapit/roadmaps/